TWINDERELLA

A FRACTIONED
Fairy Tale

Corey Rosen Schwartz • PICTURES BY Deborah Marcero

G. P. PUTNAM'S SONS

To Ella and Maya,
my favorite princess sisters
—C.R.S.

To Danielle Smith
—D.M.

G. P. PUTNAM'S SONS

an imprint of Penguin Random House LLC

375 Hudson Street

New York, NY 10014

Text copyright © 2017 by Corey Rosen Schwartz. Illustrations copyright © 2017 by Deborah Marcero.

Penguin supports copyright. Copyright fuels creativity, encourages diverse voices, promotes free speech, and creates a vibrant culture.

Thank you for buying an authorized edition of this book and for complying with copyright laws by not reproducing, scanning, or distributing

any part of it in any form without permission. You are supporting writers and allowing Penguin to continue to publish books for every reader.

G. P. Putnam's Sons is a registered trademark of Penguin Random House LLC.

Library of Congress Cataloging-in-Publication Data is available upon request.

Manufactured in China by RR Donnelley Asia Printing Solutions Ltd.

ISBN 9780399176333

10 9 8 7 6 5 4 3 2 1

Design by Marikka Tamura. Text set in Polymer.

The artwork in this book was rendered with India ink, gouache, watercolor and Photoshop.

PROLOGUE

Most of you have heard the story of Cinderella.
But you don't know the *half* of it!
Cinderella had a twin sister named Tinderella.

Here is the *whole* story . . .

Cinderella

Tinderella

Once upon a wicked time,
two sisters were mistreated.
Given lengthy lists of chores
that had to be completed.

THEY'D EACH DO:

Half the mopping,
half the raking,

half the shopping,
chopping, baking.

Half the folding,   half the mending,

half the mean
stepsister tending.

Late at night,
the weary twins
would split a
slice of bread,

share some scraps,
and then collapse
and squeeze in
half a bed.

Cin would fall asleep at once
and dream she'd found a groom.

Tin would toss and count some sheep
and wish for twice the room.

Their lives were just an endless sea
of duties to divide.
Until Prince Charming threw a ball
to find himself a bride!

IF YOU'RE SINGLE
PLEASE COME MINGLE
AT THE ROYAL BALL
WHEN: TONIGHT AT 8PM
WHERE: THE BANQUET HALL

Cin said, "Oh!
We've gotta go!
I'd love to be the queen."

"You *can't* attend,"
their stepmom sneered.
"You must stay here
and clean!"

So Cinderella grabbed a broom,
but as she started sweeping,
she felt her dreams all turn to dust
and couldn't keep from weeping.

Just then, their fairy godmom came.

I'm here to do your bidding.

Whooosh!

Tin said, "That was not half bad!"
and quickly did the splitting.

THEY EACH GOT:

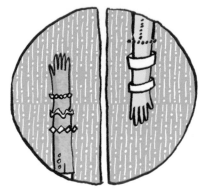 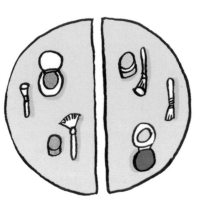 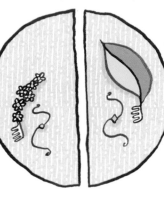  

Half the bracelets, half the blushes, half the trinkets, bows, and brushes.

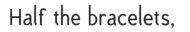

Half a coach—
they had to share.

The twins arrived at half past eight,
their faces bright and beaming.

Prince Charming did a double take.
"Gadzooks, I must be dreaming!"

The prince approached the twins at once,
enchanted by the sight.
No other girl stood half a chance—
he danced with them all night.

THEY EACH DID:

Half the zipping,
skipping, whirling.

Half the twisting,
half the twirling.

Half the swaying,
half the dipping,

half the sparkly
cider sipping.

When the clock began to chime,
the twins said, "That's our cue."

The smitten prince was left bereft,
with nothing . . . but a shoe.

He slipped the shoe on every girl
around the village square.
None fit until, at last, he hit
upon the matching pair.

"I'm so confused. *You've* got to choose!"
He looked from Cin to Tin.
Then Tin said, "Hey, there is a way
that *both* of us can win!"

She called their fairy godmother
and told her of their trouble.

$$C + T = P + X$$

$$X = ?$$

Cin	X
Tin	P.C.

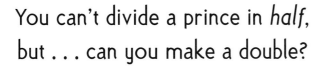

You can't divide a prince in *half*,
but . . . can you make a double?

Cin said, "If she makes a twin,
he'd have to be an heir."
She looked the prince right in the eye.
"Are you prepared to share?"

Prince Charming crossed his heart and swore
to split things even steven.
"I'd gladly give up *all* my stuff.
It's *love* that I believe in."

The prince's twin was quite a whiz
at splitting things in half—
he divvied up the royal wealth,
the crowns and loyal staff.

Tin was wowed! She told her sis,
"I love that he's so smart.
He's kind and cute and can compute!
He's wholly won my heart."

So Cin and Charming wed at once
and wound up on the throne.
And Tin? She wed the prince's twin.
That's why she's less well known.

The reigning couple kept the peace and met with dukes and lords.

The other pair won all the kingdom's highest math awards!

Cin gave birth, a baby boy,
while Tin, against all odds,

had little girls, not two or three—
the twin delivered quads!